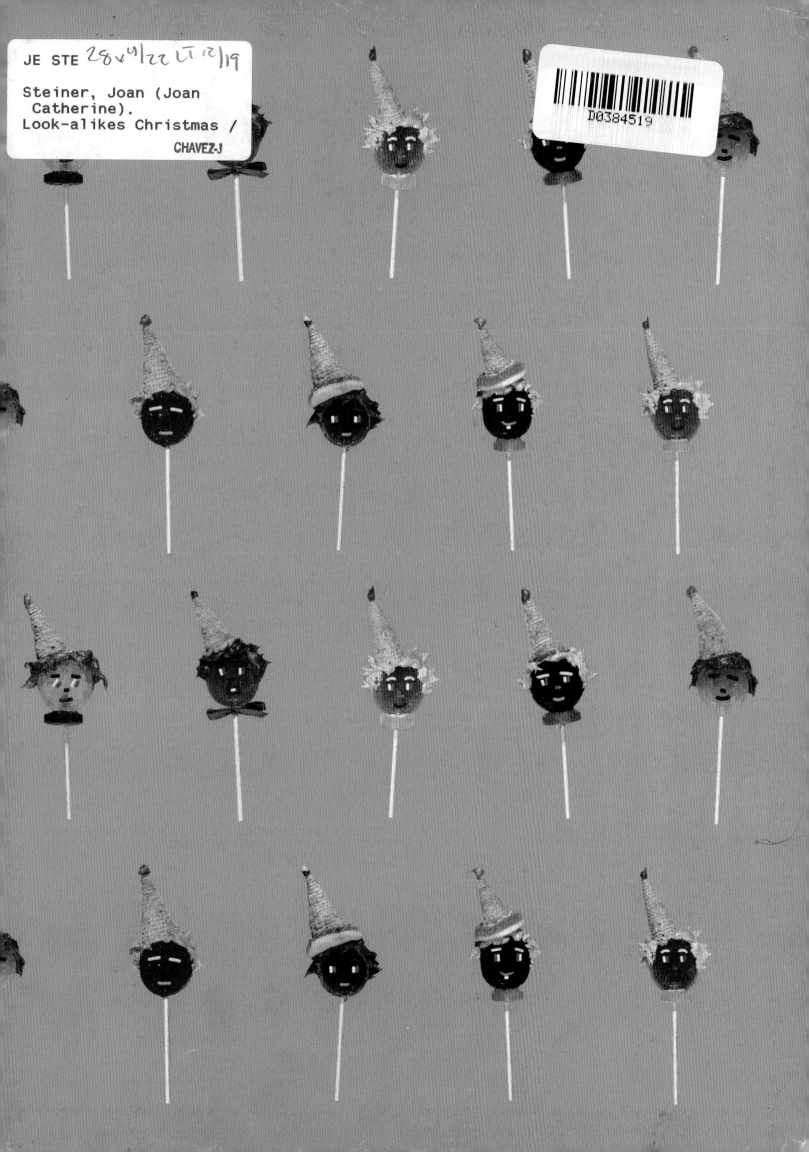

JOAN STEINER

LOOK-ALIKES

Christmas

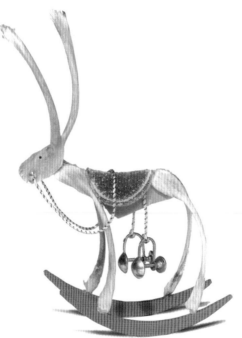

Photography by Ogden Gigli

Megan Tingley Books

LITTLE, BROWN AND COMPANY

New York · An AOL Time Warner Company

For Benny

I would like to thank my editor, Megan Tingley, and my agent, Amy Berkower, for their unflagging support, enthusiasm, patience, and excellent advice. They are both extraordinary, and I am very fortunate to be working with them. I am grateful to photographer Ogden Gigli for the artistry and eternal good humor that he brought to this very challenging assignment. Most special thanks go to my friend, the wonderful poet Joan Murray, without whom the verses would not be what they are. I am grateful to designer Billy Kelly, who worked so hard to pull this book together—a huge task—in a very short time. Stephen Blauweiss launched the fireworks into the New Year's sky, very generously giving me the benefit of his computer knowledge and technical expertise. I would also like to thank Susan Gigli, Julia Doyle, and the Ben Eaton family, who were so willing to help. Finally, my love and thanks go to my husband, George Rodenhausen, who did everything in his power to help me get the job done.

—J.S.

PHOTOGRAPHY CREDITS
All Look-Alikes® photographed by Ogden Gigli with the exception of "Grandma's Kitchen"
(Walter Wick, photographer). The candid shots in "Behind the Scenes" are by photographer
Michael Fredericks.

First Edition

Look-Alikes® is a registered trademark of Joan Steiner.

Library of Congress Cataloging-in-Publication Data

Steiner, Joan (Joan Catherine).
Look-alikes Christmas / Joan Steiner.—1st ed.
p. cm.
"Megan Tingley Books."
Summary: Simple verses challenge readers to identify the everyday objects used to construct nine
three-dimensional Christmas scenes, including a cathedral, Nutcracker ballet, and Santa's workshop. Includes
an interview with the artist and instructions for making "Look-Alikes" Christmas decorations.
ISBN 0-316-81187-4
1. Picture puzzles—Juvenile literature. 2. Christmas—Miscellanea—Juvenile literature.
[1. Picture puzzles. 2. Christmas—Miscellanea.] I. Title.

GV1507.P4S745 2003
793.73—dc21   2003047406

10 9 8 7 6 5 4 3 2 1

PHX

Printed in the United States of America

The illustrations in this book are photographs of three-dimensional constructions created from found objects.
The text was set in Xavier Sans and the display type is set in Albertus MT and Nicolas Cochin.

A t Christmastime, we love the gifts
That come as a surprise,
And if you look inside this book
You won't believe your eyes:
For all the things you thought you knew
Appear in some disguise. . . .

At least one hundred objects
To discover in each scene:
It's hours of fun for everyone—
Young, old, or in-between.
(You'll find all listed at the end
—each jack and jellybean.)

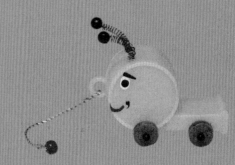

So set your imagination free—
The more you look, the more you see!

Winter Wonderland

When the snow of December makes all the world new,
It's time for a sleigh ride—in dolly's new shoe.

The Nutcracker

The *Nutcracker* ballerina is poised on her toes.
She returns every winter—yet she's fresh as a rose.

Santa's Workshop

Santa's elves are working, they're as busy as bees—
Drilling holes with noodles and making boards from cheese.

Grandma's Kitchen

Grandma's baking cookies to ward off winter's chill.
They're crisp, just like her apron—a brand new dollar bill.

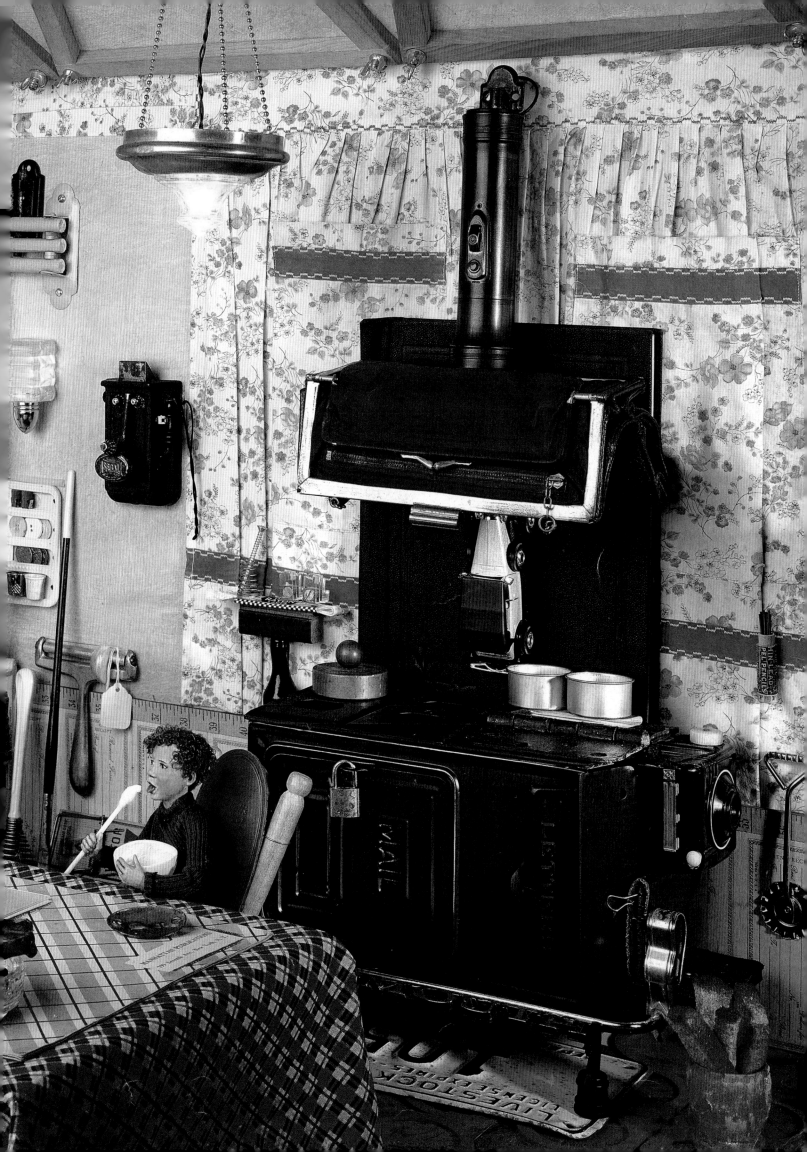

Christmas Windows

When store windows sparkle, the kids and Dad just love
To go shopping with Mom—whose coat fits like a glove.

NORTH POLE

TO FROM SANTA'S HELPERS

Cathedral

The cathedral will fill on Christmas Eve night
With the songs of the choir—and lollipop light.

Dollhouse

Santa brought a dollhouse, and the dolls will be well-fed—
They'll have snacks on the sofa and waffles in bed.

Toy Train

Santa brought a toy train, too—see it circling up ahead—
With its headlight set to guide it through a tunnel made of bread.

STATION

New Year's Eve

The bursting of fireworks brought forth a big cheer—
When the hands of the grapefruit announced the New Year!

How to Make Your Own Christmas Look-Alikes
Now you can learn to be an elf
And make amazing gifts yourself!

Peanutty Bear Ornaments
Peanuts look like teddy bears? Yes, they do!

You will need: peanuts (in shells), fine-point marker, glue gun (low-temp "hot" glue okay), small scissors, white glue (Elmer's®, Tacky™, etc.), tweezers, thin cord, and very narrow ribbon or yarn.

Adult supervision is required for this activity.

1   Carefully select peanuts that will give the look you want. A single-nut peanut works best for the head.

2   Draw a face on the head with a fine-point marker.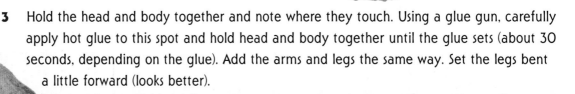

3   Hold the head and body together and note where they touch. Using a glue gun, carefully apply hot glue to this spot and hold head and body together until the glue sets (about 30 seconds, depending on the glue). Add the arms and legs the same way. Set the legs bent a little forward (looks better).

4   For ears (optional), break a peanut open and, with small scissors, cut off a very small eye-shaped piece from the rounded end of the half shell. (Some shells may crumble when you do this, but some will work.) Trim the little piece, if necessary, and glue ears on with white glue. Let set. Tweezers can make it easier to hold the ears. Eat leftover peanuts. (You could also cut a tiny piece of tan leather for the ears, or leave ears off entirely.)

5   Cut a piece of thin cord about 12" long and tie a little loop in the middle of the cord.

6   Put a thin stripe of hot glue from top of bear's head down to his neck and attach the cord, with the knot on top.

7   Put another little stripe of glue about ½ inch long from neck down bear's back and attach more of the cord. Trim off remaining cord. Don't combine steps 6 and 7.

8   Cut about 12" of very narrow ribbon or yarn. Attach ribbon to back of bear's neck with a dab of hot glue. Tie as tiny a bow as you can under bear's chin and trim off the ends of the ribbon.

9   Your bear will be somewhat fragile, so handle carefully. If a peanut breaks off, it can easily be glued back on again. (Peel off old glue first.)

Edible Elves

A popular snack food looks like elves' hats!

You will need: Bugles® snack food, flat lollipops, rainbow sprinkles, icing, cotton swab or paintbrush, craft stick or dull knife, gummi rings (optional), LifeSavers® candy (optional), and tweezers.

Recipe for icing:
- 2 egg whites
- ½ tsp. cream of tartar
- about 3½ cups powdered sugar (a little less than a box)
- food coloring or cocoa

In a large bowl, beat all ingredients together until stiff, and keep covered.
You can tint the icing with a few drops of food coloring. For brown, use cocoa.
To make stiffer, let air dry a little or add a little more sugar. To soften, add a few drops of water.

1 Moisten one side of lollipop with a wet cotton swab or paintbrush to make candy sticky. (Okay, you may moisten by licking, but only if you plan to eat the lollipop yourself!)

2 Using tweezers, position sprinkles to make a face, and let dry. Or you may simply paint a face with food coloring and a fine brush.

3 Mix up icing colors. Icing should be a consistency that spreads easily but still stiff enough to form little peaks.

4 Apply icing to lollipop with craft stick or dull knife to make funny hair.

5 While hair is still wet, stick a Bugle on head. Before putting hat on, you can make a pom-pom at the end with a little icing. You can also give the hat a "brim" either by coating the rim of the Bugle with a contrasting color of icing before putting it on head, or by first putting on a gummi ring and then sticking Bugle to that with more icing.

6 If you wish to give your elf a collar, put a little icing at the top of the lollipop stick and smush on a LifeSaver. (Or you may want to tie on a bow after the icing has set.)

7 Dry upright and do not handle until icing has set. A good way to keep the elves upright is to poke holes in an upside down egg carton.

8 Even when dry, try not to handle the elves by their hair or hat. (You wouldn't like it either!)

Cathedral Window Ornaments

Citrus slices look like cathedral windows!

You will need: sharp knife, fork, chopstick or straw, thin ribbon or cord, and the following ingredients:

- 4 cups flour
- ½ tsp. ginger
- 1 tsp. baking powder
- dried citrus slices
- ½ cup butter, melted and cooled
- brown icing (see recipe on previous page)
- Hershey's® chocolate bar and Hugs (optional)

- 1 cup molasses
- 1½ tsp. salt
- ¼ cup milk

Adult supervision is required for this activity.

Larger pattern for orange slice cookie.
Smaller pattern for lemon or lime.

1 **At least** *two weeks* **in advance,** slice lemons, limes, or small oranges crosswise to make ¼-inch- to ⅛-inch-thick slices. Place on rack or screen in warm, airy place to dry. They will shrink and the rind will get hard. (Slice more than you need, because some will dry funny.)

2 Combine flour, ginger, molasses, butter, baking powder, salt, and milk in large bowl. Chill.

3 Roll out dough to a thickness of ³⁄₁₆ to ¼ inch on greased cookie sheet.

4 Lay greased pattern on top of dough and trace outline with a sharp knife. Peel away surrounding dough. (Dough can be reused.)

5 Using fork and flat edge of knife, press decorative designs into dough as shown.

6 Make hole at top for hanging (not too close to the edge) with chopstick or straw.

7 Place a dried citrus slice on top of dough where the window will go. With sharp knife, trace the outline of the citrus slice and remove dough from window area. Set citrus slice aside. (Try to keep track of which slice goes with which cookie, as each is slightly different in shape and size.)

8 In preheated 350° oven, bake about 15 minutes, more or less depending on thickness.

9 With spatula, immediately transfer cookies from baking sheet to cooling rack.

10 When cool, make a rim of brown icing around window hole and press on citrus slice. Icing will hold slice in place.

11 Optional: For doors, put some icing on backs of chocolate squares and press onto cookies.

12 For optional awning, "slice" a Hershey's Hug in half lengthwise by gradually shaving away one side of the Hug with a sharp knife. "Glue" remaining half over door with icing. Eat the shavings.

13 When icing has set, tie on a thin ribbon or cord as shown for hanging in window.

14 Until the citrus slices are 100 percent dry, keep cookies in an airy place. And if your cathedral has chocolate doors, don't hang it above a heater!

For lemon or lime slice cookie.

Behind the Scenes:

A Sneak Peek at the Making of *Look-Alikes® Christmas*

Q: Where do you get your ideas?

A: I've always had a knack for noticing that one thing looks like another. For example, one time I was slicing lemons and I noticed how pretty they looked when held up to the light, and the segments made me think of church windows and the divisions of a clock face. This led to the grapefruit clock tower in the New Year's scene and to the idea for the cathedral cookies.

These "eureka!" moments are great, but most of the time I have to work harder to get my ideas. I take photos, look at pictures in books, shop a lot, and examine objects closely from every angle. I might spend ten minutes in a store checking out each individual Cheez Doodle through the cellophane, trying to decide if it might work. I wind up with a table covered with all sorts of objects to be considered and begin building the scene from there.

Q: You must have a studio full of stuff. Where do you get the things you use?

A: Hardware stores, supermarkets, yard sales, my own cupboards—I even pick up good things from the ground (bottle caps, maple seeds) or coffee shops (sugar packets to use for cushions). Sometimes I have to go to great lengths to get just the right thing. For the curtains in the *Nutcracker* scene, I went to a special store that sells wigs, and then, after trying unsuccessfully about five times to dye the hair the right color, I finally had to take the hair to a beauty parlor for help.

In my studio I have boxes and boxes and boxes of stuff, all packed according to categories—school supplies, games, toys, hardware, etc.—and subcategories (in "hardware," for example: things to measure with, clothespins, funnels, small tools, mousetraps, and so on). I don't know just how many thousands of objects I have in my studio, plus in a little room in my house also stuffed with my odd "art supplies." I *do* know that I could have the world's greatest yard sale!

Q: How big are the scenes and how long do they take to create?

A: Some people think Look-Alikes involve trick photography or computer manipulation. I wish! They really are painstakingly constructed of everyday objects just as they appear. Most wind up measuring around four or five feet across. You can often judge for yourself from the objects in the scene; there usually is a yardstick or ruler in there.

There's a lot of construction behind the scenes to hold all the Look-Alikes in place. They look very different on the side

that *doesn't* face the camera! To hold everything together, I use five or six different kinds of glue, plus tape, wire, thread—even gingerbread icing! Once the scene is built, it still has to be taken to the photographer and shot.

As for how long the scenes take—FOREVER! I'm a little embarrassed about how long things take me and about being such a perfectionist. But I'm also glad people ask me this, because it means they realize there's a lot of work involved. *Look-Alikes®️ Christmas* took me about three and a half years.

Q: What is the most unusual thing you've ever used? The most difficult to work with?

A: I used actual deer vertebrae for the arches in the cathedral scene in *Look-Alikes®️ Christmas.* I've also used a hand grenade and my daughter's baby teeth.

The most difficult thing to work with is FOOD. It's messy, greasy, and hard to glue. (Try gluing a Cheez Doodle—impossible!) Plus, my cats are always sneaking in and eating the artwork! On the other hand, sometimes there just might happen to be some pretzels left over for me. . . .

Q: What is your favorite scene in *Look-Alikes®️ Christmas*?

A: I'm very happy with the way all the scenes turned out, but I think I'm proudest of the cathedral because it was the biggest challenge. It was a monster to build—much bigger and heavier than most of the others, yet it had all that delicate "stained glass" (all kinds of objects plus colored paper—not very stable). It came apart and had to be put back together more than once. And it's the only scene where I got to explore the effect of light shining through colorful, translucent objects. (Usually, these are just the kind of objects that *don't* look right.) That was actually my inspiration for this piece.

In terms of a challenge, the New Year's scene is a close runner-up. Those fireworks!

Q: What inspired you to do a Christmas book?

A: I always wanted to, ever since I began with *Look-Alikes.* Maybe it's because it's such a colorful time with lots of happy associations. From a look-alike point of view, there's lots of variety in the familiar Christmas images—indoor, outdoor, day, night—and that gives me the opportunity to use a greater variety of objects and to use them in new ways. I wouldn't want to repeat myself!

EXTRA CHALLENGE

When everything's found, can a puzzle remain?

Yes, one final challenge to jingle the brain:

In each of the scenes is the same single thing—

Not to slip on a finger, though still it might "ring."

Go back now and find it—it's shiny and round.

When a horse pulls a sleigh, you might hear its sound.

HOW TO COUNT THE LOOK-ALIKES

1. If more than one of the same object is used to make up *one* look-alike—such as ten pencils making up a fence—it counts as *one* look-alike. But if the same or a similar object appears elsewhere in the scene to make a *different* look-alike—such as a pencil appearing as a flagpole—it counts again. (Brackets around an item in the list indicate that this object, used in this way, has already been identified in another part of the scene and should not be counted again.)

2. Miniatures don't count as look-alikes unless they appear as something different from a larger version of themselves. For example, a toy car that represents a real car is not a look-alike, but a toy car that looks like a fire hydrant *does* count.

3. As long as you can identify an object, you don't have to get the name exactly right.

THE LOOK-ALIKES

Asterisks indicate hard-to-find items—for super-sleuths only!

Winter Wonderland

☛ *101 Look-Alikes*

FIGURES AND SLEIGH: Corn kernels, paper clips, pistachio nut, kidney beans*, wishbones, peanut, doll shoe, striped twistie. **FOREGROUND BUILDINGS:** Pencil-tip erasers, spiral pad, pink erasers, party noisemaker, red hair clip, jingle bell, alphabet blocks, supermarket bonus stamps, small bar of soap (hotel size), electric switch plates, dog biscuit, candy canes, pasta wheels, dollhouse chair, white buckle. **FOREGROUND SCENERY, LEFT TO RIGHT:** Doilies, paper cutout snowflakes, antlers with skull bone, tiny seashells, Styrofoam packing "peanuts," various artificial flowers (all counted as one), European-style (lumpy) sugar cubes, white buttons, comb, glazed donut, tiny rabbit, aspirins, postage stamp, pencil, iced gingerbread cookie, cottage cheese (in road), tiny bear, Styrofoam divided dinner plates, valentine heart candy, cinnamon sticks, mini marshmallows, yogurt-covered pretzels, disposable razors (ski lift), skirt fasteners, white crayon, wishbones (tree), sand dollar, coconut pieces, pinecones, sunflower seeds, doorstop, button*, pieces of raccoon fur, frosted mini-wheat cereal, coffee beans, eye mask, gray scallop shell, pieces of broken glass, cauliflower, lace, white and green knitted gloves. **MIDDLE DISTANCE, LEFT TO RIGHT:** Sea sponge, pillow in pillowcase, powder puffs/makeup applicators, tiny tea box, starfish, fox fur, asparagus, [pinecones], white coral, matches, picture hook, artist's palette, jacks, two change purses, yellow buckle, (artificial) lilac flower clump, (artificial) yellow flower, cake. **MOUNTAINS IN DISTANCE, LEFT TO RIGHT:** Eggshells, bra, Halloween skeleton, garlic clove, clam shell, chenille toy cat, toy horse, cotton balls, plaster face in profile, gray sneakers, marshmallow chicks, white sneaker, antlers, three white gloves, child's sock, feather bird, child's cap, plush cat, white onions, hand towel.

The Nutcracker

☞ *122 Look-Alikes*

PROSCENIUM AND CURTAINS: Gold chain, gold lace, carpenter's folding rule, jingle bells, gold belts, keys, picture hangers, birthday candles, banana peels, corn kernels, real hair, barrettes, coin purses, pen nibs, angel-wing cookies, strawberry Twizzlers. **DANCERS: Blue Soldier and Sentry Box:** ballet slipper, buckle, striped birthday candle, pencils, padlock, toothbrushes, safety pin, jelly beans, old-fashioned key. **Maid:** peppermint candy, guitar pick, scallop shell. **Godfather and His Gifts:** nacho chips, eyeglass cases, popcorn, (artificial) grapes, seashells (hats), wishbone, (artificial) rose, balloons, wax candy bottles, bangle bracelet. **Clara and Her Nutcracker's Bed:** badminton birdie, spiral pasta, bar of soap, wooden matches. **Red Soldier:** nail polish, ballpoint pen tops, [two jelly beans]. **CHRISTMAS TREE:** Candy corn, dried fern, gold necklaces, safety pins, M&M's, buttons, jelly beans, thumbtacks, aspirin*, tiny seashell, bingo call number, pearl beads, silver snaps, bolt, corn kernel, baby tooth, zipper slider, nut (nuts-and-bolts type), pearl earring. **GIFTS UNDER TREE:** Pasta bow tie, ball-headed pins, spool of thread (drum), spools of thread (cylindrical wrapped gifts), bouillon cubes, alphabet blocks, dice, gold candy coin, box of matches, Lego piece, cauliflower, tassel, chess knight, barrettes, cough drop. **CHANDELIERS:** Ponytail elastics, light chain pulls. **BACKGROUND SCENERY:** Pea pods, red flowers, nutcracker, cap-gun caps, chess pawns, recorders, cotton swabs, crayons, seed packet, Nestlé Crunch bars, green cookies, brass paper fasteners, penny, ring, playing cards, baby bottle nipple, broccoli, overalls buckle, clothespins, telephone cords, marbles, golf tees, brass nuts (nuts-and-bolts type), hair scrunchies, cocktail forks, play money, candy canes. **Objects Seen Through Windows:** saltshaker, onion*, Christmas ball, opera glasses, votive candle. **Owl and Clock:** button, maple seeds, almond, pastry cutter, zipper sliders, sewing needle, gold coin, Scrabble tile. **FLOOR:** Desk blotter, gumdrops (footlights).

Santa's Workshop

☞ *168 Look-Alikes*

Note: All buttons used as wheels *count once.*

THE ELVES: Two Elves and Worktable on Left: nose mask, spiral seashell, rolled-up pair of socks, peanuts, tortilla chip, baby shoe, circus peanuts, dog biscuits, wooden match, pool cue chalk, spool of pink thread, spiral pasta (drills), buttons, wrapped stick of gum, larger dog biscuit (vise), golf tee, chocolate-covered wafer cookies, Triscuit crackers. **Red Elf:** pincushion with pins and sharpening "strawberry," green ponytail elastic*, sword toothpick, dishwashing sponge, matches, tea candles. **Elf and Workbench on Right:** Gatorade bottle top, hackeysack, cheese slicer, block of cheese, coin wrappers. **CEILING:** Matzoh, pretzel rods, golf club, shredded wheat, rulers, wooden hangers (ceiling trusses)*. **LEFT-HAND WALL, TOP TO**

BOTTOM: Tortoiseshell hair clip, pecans, knife sheath, clothespins, pink party noisemaker, [buttons], waffle, caramels, fig bar, dried maple seed, crayons, ticket, animal crackers, slice of lime, striped birthday candles, small red potato, yellow ponytail elastic, brown potato (mailbag). **BACK WALL:** Full-size wooden chair. **Shelves on Left:** wooden flute, cherry tomato, Brazil nut, red plastic wall hook, [buttons], spool of thread, hair curler, pushpin, doll shoe, snaps*, lighter, M&M's, chess knight, barrettes, peanuts, acorn, spiral pasta, British flag, leather wallet. **Between Shelves and Hallway:** cinnamon sticks, bingo call letter, picture block, dog biscuits* (bench). **Hallway:** toy baby bottle, brass hinges, banana chips, pepper mill, candy cane, crocheted change purse, Hershey's Kiss (red foil), screw, wrapped coughdrop, Milky Way bars, tea bag, Jacob's ladder. **Fireplace:** red kidney beans, penny, clock minute hand*, gum eraser, biscotti, Christmas ball, chess pawns, large safety pin, croutons, guitar picks (bellows). **Right-Hand Shelves:** corncob pipes, Cheerios, bouillon cubes (in two places), spiral pasta, pistachio nut, corn kernel, whistle, red die, jingle bell, candy corn, AA battery, [buttons], matchbox, tassel, artificial flowers (doll), pencil sharpener, dreidel, real moth, child's barrette, guitar pick, sewing needle* (sailboat mast), alphabet blocks, (artificial) white flower (package bow), Bic lighter, sewing needle* (trim on truck), [spool of thread], wrapped fruit candy, chopsticks, chocolate biscuits. **Green Cupboard Area:** pecans, pencils, green pencil-tip erasers, wrapped caramel, tray from box of chocolates, dice, spool of green thread (drum), ball-headed pins, thimble, fake fingernail, caramel (purse), roll caps, diary, spool of pink thread, wooden yardsticks, marshmallow Easter chick. **RIGHT-HAND WALL:** Vegetarian "bacon." **Stove:** lipstick case, mini flashlight, camera lens, pushpins, jelly jar lid, bingo card. **Shelf:** doll boots, wrapped bar of soap, eraser, [die]. **ON FLOOR:** Potholders. **Scooter:** sticks of gum, birthday candle, [buttons]. **Reindeer:** three wishbones, fruit-slice candy, earring backs. **Dollhouse:** two books of matches, orange envelope, buttons, supermarket stamps, white birthday candles, pearl buckle. **Wrapped Gifts:** bubblegum in wrapper, Scrabble tiles, [picture block]. **Doll Furniture:** green dog biscuits, cookie, postage stamp, spiral pasta.

Grandma's Kitchen

☛ *153 Look-Alikes*

PEOPLE: Dollar bill, white seashell, cotton swab. **TABLE AND CHAIRS:** Tiny slate, piece of chalk, aspirin tin with aspirins, sheet music, cigar holder, glass ashtray, brass keyhole, clothespins, two wallets, heel cushion (boy's chair). **PANTRY:** Carpenter's rule, pencils, sink plug, marble, gum eraser, old-fashioned box (of nails), egg carton, whistle, dice, round eraser with brush, glass fuse, blue coral*, socket adapter, pussy willow, garter, tiny battery, bottle cap, pinecone, bell, dental floss, crayons, toggle button, Lego piece, spools, wooden pestle, Tinkertoy piece, [box of nails], wooden ice cream spoon, hinge*, stencil. **GREEN CUPBOARD:** Retractable tape measure, champagne cork cage, pencil sharpener, compass, coin, fuse, silver nuts (nuts-and-bolts type), toy truck, cigarette lighter, cigarette rolling papers, pencil sharpener, votive candle, pushpin, jingle bell, coin wrappers, shade pull, compressed peat pot (also called a "jiffy pot"), upside-down sugar bowl lid, calendar of checkbook register, tire gauge, recipe pamphlet. **ITEMS ON GREEN WALL:** Card with snaps, suction cup, brass paper fastener*, cocktail fork, toy pilot's wings, knife, electric plug adapter, old-fashioned skate key, pants hanger, shower curtain hook, red game piece*, Scrabble tiles, bottle cap, [gum eraser], saltshaker top, pretzels, Scrabble tray, window latch, champagne cork cage, spiral pasta, corncob holder, Bell's Seasoning box. **SINK AREA:** Small clasp envelopes, soap dish, pick comb, box of pencil leads, *Farmer's Almanac*, wrench, black game piece, can/bottle opener, old-fashioned key, white plastic buckle, pencil-tip eraser, bobby pins. **CEILING:** Old-fashioned tennis racquet presses, coffee pot lid (hanging). **ITEMS ON PINK WALL:** Apron. **Window Area:** three-bar towel rack, package carrying handle, window latch, alphabet block, door bolt, nylon gloves, broccoli. **To Right of Window:** saltshaker, birthday candle, coin holder, mechanical pencil erasers, buttons, dimes, thimble, toothpaste tube cap, cheese slicer, garlic clove*, price tag. **Telephone:** black door lock, drill chuck key, snaps, chess pawn*. **Shelf Left of Stove:** rubber stamp, spring, brass screw, clear mirror brackets, shoelaces in wrapper. **To Right of Stove:** container of pencil leads, ravioli cutter. **ALONG LOWER WALL:** Tape measure, receipts, whisk, paintbrush, mousetrap. **STOVE:** Door-bolt receptacle, flashlight, black notebook, old-fashioned purse, toy car, brass paperweight, black light switch plates, oil paint solvent cups, black hinge, mailbox with lock, old-fashioned Brownie camera, leather keyholder, clip-on chrome towel bar, chrome word "Plymouth" from a car*, black chess knight*. **ON FLOOR:** License plate, egg cup, toast slices, rubber canning rings, linen napkin (to left of table).

Christmas Windows

☞ 117 Look-Alikes

THE PEOPLE: Left of Center: sea urchin shell, baby tooth, pinecones, liquor bottle stopper, alphabet noodles, safety pins, gumdrop, fondue forks (tripod), upside-down bell, cell phone, dried apricot, tiny pinecone* (woman's hair), knit glove, paper clip, small spools of thread, tiny padlock, orange ponytail elastic, (artificial) ferns, Cheez Doodle, circus peanuts, orange thimbles, frog finger puppet. **Right of Center:** spiral seashell, silver snap, potato, Fig Newton, wine corks, saltshaker top, silk change purse, sticks of clay*, jelly beans, mini marshmallows* (child's boot tops), tassel, rolled-up socks, domino, small soap, Chinese finger traps, [ponytail elastic], Styrofoam packing "peanuts", wrapped chocolate, woven leather button, Chinese fried noodle, playing cards, tiny basket, cookie, peanuts, loofah, pepper packets, postage stamp, cigarillos (type of cigar). **WINDOW ON LEFT:** Upside-down basket, gum eraser, twig doll's chair, dog biscuits, peanuts, cinnamon stick*, magnet, almond, grape stems (antlers), wooden buckle, little blue goose, LifeSavers candy, red thimble, tape dispenser, figs, butter knives, curved sewing needles*, rolling pin, gift tag, fruit-slice candy, white feathers, gummi apple rings, spiral cookie. **WINDOW ON RIGHT:** [cinnamon sticks, feathers, rolling pin, and gift tag], strand of mini lights, matzoh, red LifeSavers candy, green fruit-slice candy, parakeet perch, Twizzler candy, wooden flute, breadsticks, red plastic squeezable coin purse, tea bag, eye-makeup applicators. **DEPARTMENT STORE EXTERIOR:** Sandwich cookie, baseball cap, gold tiaras, jingle bells (on canopy), plastic protractor, tea candle, hoop earring, lantern, ruler*, backscratchers, dog biscuits, jingle bells (trim on columns), sergeant's stripes, (artificial) melon quarters, tape measure, towel bars, chocolate coins. **BUILDING ON RIGHT:** Pencils, chopsticks in wrapper, tray from box of chocolates, door chain lock, cigar box, gold hoop earring*, washboard, pipe cleaner, wooden cocktail forks, cheesy crackers, gold barrette*, ruler. **STREET LIGHTS:** Necklaces, coat hook, saltshaker, mini paper candy cup, egg (hollowed out, lit from within).

Cathedral

☞ 110 Look-Alikes

WINDOW ON LEFT: Top: rope, gas-range burner ring, sunglasses, plastic spiders, plastic spider web (Halloween decoration), pretzels, artificial flowers, plastic lizards, fireplace pokers, rotary phone dials. **Side Panels:** lollipops, ponytail elastics, toothbrushes. **Picture Panel on Left:** celery slice*, clear push-pin, plastic letters A and H, supermarket stamp, hair comb, bread package closure tag, eye (hook-and-eye type), buckle, birthday candle, tea bag, false eyelash, shoehorn, fake fingernails, purple plastic ring, maple seeds, scallop shell, paper clips, oak leaf, [artificial flower], jelly beans. **Picture Panel on Right:** guitar pick, pasta bow tie, fruit-slice candy, plastic grapes, gummi bears (ten in various colors), pasta wheels, Cheez Doodle, squishy fish lure, (artificial) leaf, tiny key, key chain, wax candy bottle, seahorse, feather. **Bottom Panels:** breakfast cereal, bike pedals. **Wall and Columns Surrounding Window:** real deer vertebrae, coffee filters, rice cakes, tubes from paper-towel rolls, cocktail bread slices. **SMALLER WINDOW ON RIGHT:** Embroidery hoop, butterflies, "little man" paper clips, small hair grip, whistles, wire cutters, tiny keys, shamrock stickers, automatic "click" pencils, jacks, transparent reproductions of playing cards (I cheated—the only time), [rope]. **BACK WALL:** Flat clothespins, wishbones, round clothespins (statues), bells* (two kinds, as hats), mousetraps, wooden forks, recorders, chess pieces, lace, pennies, silver salt-and-pepper caddy, alphabet blocks, golf tees, books. **IN NAVE:** Garter belt, manicure scissors, black lace, tape measures, Scrabble trays, Scrabble tiles, protractor, ice-cream cone, bullets, Chinese finger traps, sink mat. **RIGHT-HAND WALL AND VAULTED CEILING:** Dog biscuits (three sizes), curtain (the columns), tickets, stud earrings*. **Organ:** brass hinges, artist's sandpaper pad, pen nibs, overalls buckle, gold pencils. **Pulpit:** sugar bowl with lid, jingle bells, chess pawns*. **Statues:** spoon, coin, tiny perfume bottle, toy trumpet Christmas decoration, long hasp padlock, acorn, finger protector*, crayon, abacus.

Dollhouse

☛ *150 Look-Alikes*

ROOF: Mini-blinds, gum erasers. **NURSERY:** Gummi vampire teeth, pink wafer cookies, black-eyed peas, biscuit, animal crackers, gummi heart candy, chess knight, barrettes, combs, sugar and sweetener packets, sponge*, pencil-tip erasers, calendar. **BATHROOM:** Luggage tag, tiny fans (wedding favors), cards of thumbtacks, shredded wheat, dental floss, earring backs*, gummi apple ring (white side), egg cup, hotel-size soaps, picture hangers (two different places), chess castle, drinking glass, butter dish top, sheets of loose-leaf reinforcements. **UPPER HALLWAY:** Coin wrappers, green plastic produce basket, golf tees, drinking straw segment, mini paper candy cup, trumpet Christmas ornament, hourglass egg timer. **BEDROOM:** Compact, notepad, alphabet blocks, M&M's, play money, (artificial) pea pods, pencils, waffles, marzipan bananas, [sponge], bells, perfume box, gift tag, eyeglass case, spools of thread, buttons, stencils. **LIVING ROOM:** Seed packet, rulers, circus peanuts, yo-yo, peanuts, pink paper drumstick frill, nail polish, toy drum Christmas ornament, pushpins, Twizzler, pocket comb, brass drawer hardware, jacks, red whistles, red Zinger cakes, block of cheese in red wax, red licorice bites, staplers, chess pawns, miniature basket, tire pressure gauge, silver coin, playing cards, window latch, metal bookend, pretzel, hair clip. **DINING ROOM:** Individual apricot tart, small clothespins, wooden tic-tac-toe game, [golf tees and drinking straw], checkerboard cookie, sticks of gum, chess pawns, wooden switch plate, cinnamon sticks, Triscuit crackers, wooden artist's palette. **KITCHEN:** Tickets, paint chip strip, postage stamps, travel soap dish, automotive fuse, sticks of chalk*, silver belt buckle, paper clips, snaps, card of buttons, eye shadow, cotton swab, fruit-slice candy, playing card, toenail clippers, bingo cards, coin wrappers. **TURRET AND PORCH:** Tiny paper lantern, pill organizer, tissue box cover, jingle bells, birthday candles, tape dispensers, LifeSavers candies, yogurt-covered pretzel. **PATIO:** Soapdish, birdseed cup, red comb, books of matches, paper clamps, tip of pencil, little dish, coaster, scissors, palm tree cocktail stirrers, Cheez Doodles, #6 metal house numbers, dog biscuits, jigsaw puzzle (blank side). **ITEMS ON TREE:** Balloons, tomato on vine, phone cord, chili peppers, strawberries, party streamers. **Angel:** mint candy, fruit-slice candy, tortilla chip. **Teddy Bear:** peanuts. **Reindeer:** wishbones, tiny fruit-slice candy, dried orange peel*. **Candle:** candy corn, breadstick, pink gummi rings, Ritz cracker. **EASY CHAIR:** Cane, rope, blueberry pie. **ITEMS ON FLOOR:** Shower cap, wooden hanger, hacksaws, dishwashing sponge on stick.

Toy Train

☛ *121 Look-Alikes*

TRAIN, FRONT TO BACK: Lamp socket, spool of thread, brass door bolt, buckle, ball-point pen refill, safety pin, keys, metal buttons, razor-blade dispenser, snaps, harmonica, bingo call numbers, combs, leather doggy chews, toilet paper roll, pencil sharpener, blue rubber bands, crayon, silver dollars, brass paper fastener, drill-bit set, wooden matches, saltshaker, ponytail elastics, ticket, wooden clothespins, Popsicle sticks, Monopoly hotel, matchbox, plastic flags on pins. **ACCESSORIES: Track:** small bandages. **Remote Control:** playing card, Tootsie Pop, comb, mini paper candy cup, zipper pull. **Tunnel:** loaf of bread. **Trees and Bushes:** (artificial) ferns, buttons, artichokes, Ritz crackers, chewy spearmints, cinnamon stick, green carnation on comb (St. Patrick's Day hair ornament). **General Store:** plastic berry basket, green index cards, supermarket stamps, crayons, barrette, birthday candle, slate. **Barns:** Chinese soap dish, fruit-slice candy, alphabet blocks, buckle, milk carton. **Vehicles:** postage stamp, pencil sharpener, Fig Newtons, small bandage, [snaps]. **Signals and Signs:** M&M, nail file, candy cane, silver nut (nuts-and-bolts type), coin, lollipop, hose washer, magnetic letter X, pencil. **Road, Traffic Island, Pond:** dressy socks, shoe innersole, geode slice, toy snake. **Bridge:** napkin holder, dominoes. **Lamppost:** jingle bell, champagne cork cage, tiny perfume bottle, bullet, [coin]. **Station:** cigarillo tip, plastic harmonica, paper bag, waffle, part of a Hershey bar. **Cottage:** cork, purse, soap, gummi bears, potholder loom. **Extra Boxcar:** paint chip strip, crochet hooks. **Water Tower:** paper parasol, hot-beverage sleeve, wooden cocktail forks. **ON THE TREE:** Plastic Easter eggs, nuts (nuts-and-bolts type), spiral pasta (garland), gumdrops, fishing float, (artificial) squash. **Jack-in-the-Box:** almond, mint candy, ponytail elastics, alphabet block. **Elf:** Hershey's Kiss, hazelnut, candy canes, circus peanut, jelly beans. GIFTS UNDER TREE: Alphabet blocks (giftwrap), apple, spiral pasta (bow), book, brick. **WALL AND FIREPLACE:** Tickets*, yardsticks, wooden forks, breadsticks, black plastic cooking spoons, baguettes, composition pads.

New Year's Eve

☞ *102 Look-Alikes*

FIREWORKS: Tufts of white pine, feathers, ornamental grass seed head (fluffy), (artificial) pink Queen Anne's lace, dried dill seed head. (Yes, the fireworks were photographed separately!) **BUILDINGS FROM LEFT TO RIGHT:** Grater, crossword puzzles, model train, radiator, birdcage, washboard, protractor, suet holder, suet cakes, knife block with knife, bottle of ink, old-fashioned camera, toaster oven, eye-shadow palettes, portable cassette player with cassette, dominoes, thermos, ice-cube tray, plastic silverware tray, green crayon, wooden fork, comb, coconut cookies, chocolate squares, paper cocktail umbrella, bookend, birthday candle holders, clothing label, bingo card, power strip, computer keyboard. **Clock Tower Building:** sandwich cookies, chess pieces, small round picture frame, grapefruit slice, embroidery scissors, rulers, chopsticks, dog biscuits, pennies, cotton swabs, clothespins, wishbones, vegetable peeler, recorders, sugar shaker*, nutcracker, hourglass egg timer, alphabet block*. **To Right of Clock Tower:** lantern, candle, window blinds, striped dishtowel*, key, kitchen tongs, tool holster, jingle bells, drafting compass, knives, nutcracker, iron rest, buttons, snaps, watercolor paint tray, saltshakers. **STREET LAMPS AND TREES:** HAPPY NEW YEAR headband, cup hooks, bells, gold pencils, brass hose nozzles, screwdrivers, kernels of corn (star). **PEOPLE FROM LEFT TO RIGHT:** Grapefruit, pinecone, pear, knit hat with pom-pom, roll, mini "koosh" ball, sponge, small (artificial) flowers, golf tee, yellow paper clip, red spinning top, pot scrubber, whisk broom, backpack, pincushion, roll of masking tape*, pearl onion, walnut shell, coconut, muffin, small cup, Christmas light bulb, crepe paper roll, twist of embroidery floss, mini coffee-cake pastry.

Answer to Extra Challenge: jingle bell

JOAN STEINER is a graduate of Barnard College and a self-taught artist. Her two previous *Look-Alikes* books have sold more than one million copies and have been published in sixteen countries around the world. The recipient of numerous art and design awards, including a Society of Illustrators Award and a National Endowment for the Arts fellowship, Ms. Steiner lives in Claverack, New York.

ACCOLADES FOR *LOOK-ALIKES*®

A *New York Times* Notable Book of the Year · A *Time* Best Book of the Year · A *Los Angeles Times* Best Book of the Year · A *San Francisco Chronicle* Best Book of the Year · A *Publishers Weekly* Best Book of the Year · A *Parenting* Best Book of the Year · A *Child* Best Book of the Year · "Astounding." —*New York Times Book Review* · "A tour de force of trompe l'oeil . . . a work of visual genius."—*Publishers Weekly* (starred review) · "Fantastic . . . loaded with surprises." —*Kirkus* (starred review) · "An inspiration." —*The Bulletin* (starred review)

ACCOLADES FOR *LOOK-ALIKES*® *Jr.*

An Oppenheimer Toy Portfolio Platinum Book Award Winner · "[A] stellar sequel . . . In Steiner's hands, the ordinary becomes extraordinary."—*Publishers Weekly* (starred review) · "Dazzling ingenuity . . . amazing."—*Kirkus* (starred review) · "Brilliant . . . children and adults will be mesmerized." —*Booklist*

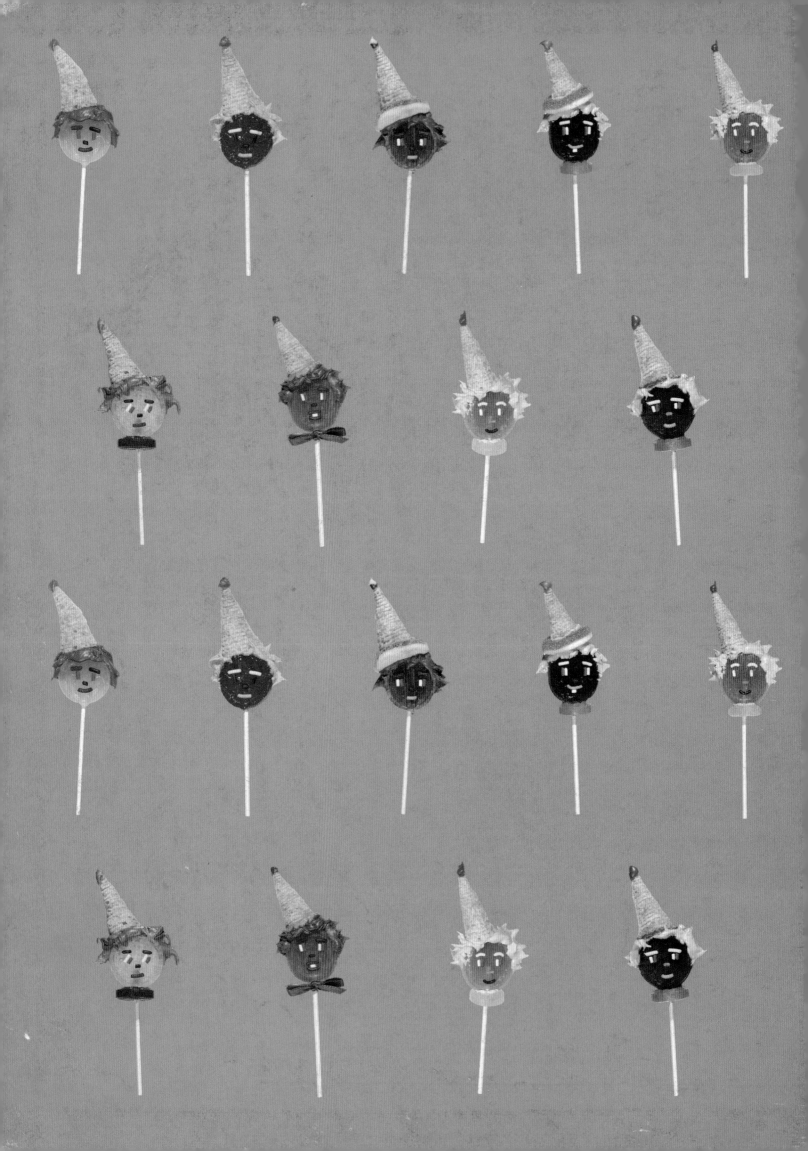